A Cigar Means Never Having to Say You're Sorry

A Cigar Means Never Having to Say You're Sorry

Jeff MacNelly

St. Martin's Press
New York

Library of Congress Cataloging-in-Publication Data
MacNelly, Jeff.
    A cigar means never having to say you're sorry.

    I. Title.
PN6728.S475M275   1989   741.5'973   88-29889
ISBN 0-312-02651-X (pbk.)

A Cigar Means Never Having to Say You're Sorry

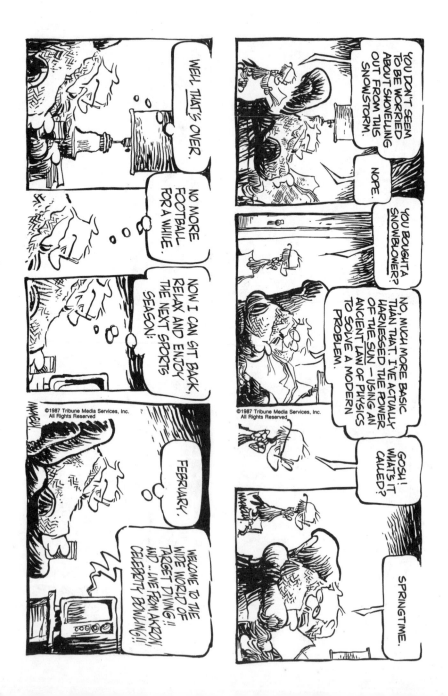

or "Basketball Scores," to the uninitiated.

Milwaukee beat New Jersey. San Antonio beat Denver.

Phoenix beat Houston. Indiana beat Utah. Philadelphia beat Sacramento.

CHOPE

By JEFF MACNELLY ®

Now for the Hoop Hype, Roundball Roundup, and Dunk Dope...

The L.A. Lakers beat the L.A. Clippers, and finally...

Cleveland beat Detroit, Seattle beat Golden State,

Portland beat New York, Dallas beat Kansas City,

THERE'S NOTHING THAT SAYS SPORTSWRITERS CAN'T BE FANS, TOO.

totally wiped out, stomped on, and otherwise uglified an out-played, demoralized Boston Celtics squad...

an inspired Chicago Bulls team, led by the incomparable Michael Jordan and his 43 points,

THEY'D SIMPLIFY THE TAX CODE BEYOND ALL COMPREHENSION.

I KNEW IT.... IF THEY PUT THEIR MINDS TO IT...

I AM INTRODUCING A BILL TO FURTHER SIMPLIFY OUR FEDERAL TAX SYSTEM...

GEE, BILLIE SOL, I WISH YOU COULD PHRASE THAT IN ANOTHER WAY...

"PUT IT ALL ON AMALGAMATED"...?

B.S.? I NEED A GOOD, SOLID, CONSERVATIVE, BLUE-CHIP STOCK TO INVEST IN...

I THINK I'LL CALL UP MY CRACK STOCKBROKER, BILLIE SOL WRIGHTOFF...

I GIVE UP! WHAT IS IT THIS TIME?
DON'T WORRY... A GOOD MECHANIC HAS TO BE A GOOD DETECTIVE, TOO.
NOW LET'S LOOK FOR A CLUE...
THE TRANSMISSION IN THE DRIVEWAY IS PROBABLY A GOOD PLACE TO START...
MACNELLY

DO YOU SEE THE PROBLEM?
I THINK SO.
WHEN YOU'VE DONE THIS AS LONG AS I HAVE, YOU GET SO'S YOU CAN LISTEN TO A CAR—IT CAN ACTUALLY TELL YOU WHAT'S WRONG...
AND YOUR CAR IS SAYING, "I'M ON FIRE."
MACNELLY

Correction:

Because of a typographical error in yesterday's edition...

the benefit dinner for Senator Belfry was unintentionally referred to as a fun-raiser.

The Tattler-Tribune regrets the error.

The 1988 Presidential race got more crowded today...

with the news that the Senator from E. Virginia,

the 354-pound Battson D. Belfry, had entered the race.

©1987 Tribune Media Services, Inc.
All Rights Reserved

©1987 Tribune Media Services, Inc.
All Rights Reserved

TTOSE WERE HIS WORDS?

YES, AND I KNOW THAT IT SOUNDS FANTASTIC...

GOD TOLD ME THAT I HAVE TO GET A RAISE...

AND IF I DIDN'T GET ONE BY THE END OF THE DAY...

..HE WOULD CALL ME HOME.

THAT WORKED MUCH BETTER FOR ORAL ROBERTS...

YOU'RE FIRED. GO HOME.

NOT AT ALL, I BELIEVE YOU.

YOU DO?

SEE THAT JUNKED '55 DESOTO OVER THERE?...

SO WE'RE TALKING ABOUT SOME SERIOUS LOONIES HERE.

THERE'S A LOT OF VERY VALUABLE STUFF IN HERE...

OKAY, SO WE GET AN OCCASIONAL JUNK-PICKER IN HERE. HOW DANGEROUS IS THAT?

THIS IS A JUNKYARD.

I SEE.

THERE ARE COLLECTORS WHO WOULD KILL FOR A HANDFUL OF PARTS OFF THAT HEAP.

YOU WANT TO LOCK IT?
NAH ... NOBODY EVER COMES NEAR TO STEALING ANYTHING OUTTA HERE.
YOU HAVE ONE OF THOSE ALARMS?
YES, A TRUCK ALARM:
-A DOBERMAN CHAINED TO THE SPARE.
©1987 Tribune Media Services, Inc. All Rights Reserved

CASH OR CHARGE?
CHARGE.
JUST A MINUTE, SIR, I'LL CALL IT IN ...
HELLO, FEDERAL RESERVE? TELL MR. GREENSPAN WE'VE FOUND THE PROBLEM.
©1987 Tribune Media Services, Inc. All Rights Reserved

GENTLEMEN OF THE PRESS ...

TRICK OR TREAT !!

SOME HALLOWE'EN COSTUMES ARE SCARIER THAN OTHERS ...

SEN. BELFRY

If you're looking for a good way to manage your time better ...

try taking a free moment early in the day...

.. and shoot your phone.

I THINK THE FILM REALLY WORKED ON TWO LEVELS...
I WOULDN'T KNOW...
DOWN IN FRONT — AT THE FLICKS WITH SHOE and the PERFESSER
I ONLY SAW IT FROM ONE LEVEL.
WE GOT KICKED OUT OF THE BALCONY FOR DRINKING BEER.
©1987 Tribune Media Services, Inc. All Rights Reserved

I NEED SOMEONE TO WRITE STRONG, HARD-HITTING EDITORIALS...
DO YOU HAVE WHAT IT TAKES?
WELL, YES AND NO...
YOU'RE HIRED.
©1987 Tribune Media Services, Inc. All Rights Reserved

SENATOR, HOW WILL YOU DEAL WITH THIS "WIMP FACTOR"?...
WIMP?
SOMEONE CALLIN' ME A WIMP?
I'M TELLIN' MY MOMMY!
©1987 Tribune Media Services, Inc. All Rights Reserved
MARGULY

YOU TELL WHOEVER IT IS WHAT IS CALLIN' ME A WIMP...
—YOU TELL HIM TO LOOK AT MY WAR RECORD!!...
LOOK AT HIS WAR RECORD.
©1987 Tribune Media Services, Inc. All Rights Reserved
MARGULY

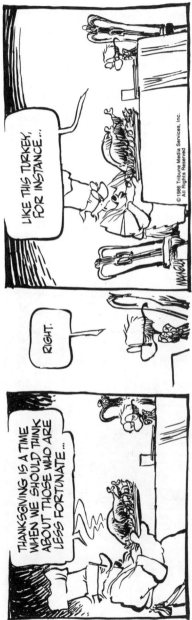

"Anyone who likes journalism, wry humor, cigars, good drawing or birds will almost certainly find that this Shoe always fits," wrote the *Washington Post* in reviewing the first collection of SHOE comic strips, drawn by three-time Pulitzer Prize winner Jeff MacNelly of the *Chicago Tribune.*

MacNelly began the comic strip, which appears in almost 1,000 newspapers, daily and Sunday, in 1977. He won his first Pulitzer Prize in 1972, his second in 1978 and a third in 1985 for his editorial cartoons. He has also won the George Polk Award and twice received the Reuben, the highest honor of The National Cartoonists Society.

A native of Cedarhurst, New York, who attended Phillips Academy of Andover, Massachusetts, MacNelly began his career drawing sports and editorial cartoons for his college paper, the *Daily Tar Heel,* at the University of North Carolina. Later, as editorial cartoonist for the town newspaper, *The Chapel Hill Weekly,* MacNelly hit his stride, spoofing the local upheavals and "ridiculosities" that characterize North Carolina politics.

His efforts earned the National Newspaper Association's 1969 award for best editorial cartooning, and the following year he became editorial cartoonist for the Richmond, Virginia, *News Leader.* In March 1982, he joined the *Chicago Tribune.* MacNelly currently resides in Washington, D.C.